My Little Island

by Frané Lessac

HarperTrophy

A Division of HarperCollins*Publishers*

My best friend, Lucca, and I are going to visit the little Caribbean island where I was born. From the air it looks like a giant green turtle swimming in the sea.

When our plane lands, we see dozens of smiling faces welcoming us.

It's good to be home again!

On the way to my aunt's house we pass dozens of brightly painted wooden houses.

From the road they look like little rainbows sitting on the hills.

As we drive up a mountainside, a breeze begins to blow. It smells so sweet.

Lucca wants to know the names of all the beautiful trees and flowers. I know only some of them: frangipani and jasmine flowers, yellow poui and red flamboyant trees, pink coral and sweet bay-rum trees.

My aunt has lunch ready for us when we arrive.

It is too hot to cook indoors, so my aunt cooked the food outside in old coal-pots.

My cousins and I gobble up pumpkin soup, pigeon peas, goat-water stew, red snapper fish, and fried bananas topped with guava ice cream.

Lucca makes funny faces but eats it all.

After lunch lots of children come to play with us. Donkeys and goats, cats and dogs, birds and cows are everywhere. We even see iguanas that are three feet long, and giant barking frogs. Our friends call the barking frogs "mountain chickens."

Lucca and I laugh.

Who will believe us back home?

"To market! To market!" my aunt sings out early the next morning.

When we get to town, the sun is just peeking over the mountaintops, but people from nearby villages are already arriving by bus, by donkey, by foot!

On their heads many people balance baskets loaded with cinnamon and fresh nutmeg and other good things to sell.

"Wha de mangoes?" "Wha de nuts?" people ask.

They want to know the prices before they buy.

Lucca and I can't decide what to get: soursops, guavas, christophines, mangoes, coconuts, or juicy orange pawpaws.

Which will taste the best?

14

By noontime it's too hot to walk around anymore.

Even the noisy traffic has stopped.

We sit down under a palm tree in the square and eat the fruits we bought at the market.

After lunch Lucca and I duck into an island shop
to buy presents for everyone back home.

We choose mango jam, guava cheese, lime
squash—and some very hot pepper sauce for
Lucca's father.

The next day we take a walk along the seashore.

Fathers and sons are rowing brightly painted wooden boats with names like *Frangelica*, *Annipani*, and *Shonabee*. They catch mackerel, parrot fish, tuna fish, trunkfish, and picasso fish in their huge nets.

When their boats are filled with flipping and flopping fish, they row back to shore.

A fisherman blows a conch shell. People hear the "Tootle-tu-whooo!" and run to the beach to buy nice, fresh fish for supper.

The afternoon is hot, hot, hot.

Lucca and I dive into the sea and spend hours snorkeling in the cool underwater world.

On Friday I take Lucca to see my old school.

The teacher lets us stay and listen to folktales and play games with tiny beads on a wooden board. We make more new friends: Sylvester, Desmond, Simon, Sylvia, Glendina, and Althea.

We promise Mrs. O'Garra to write to the class. We won't forget!

Almost everywhere we go, calypso and reggae music plays sweetly to our ears.

Lucca thinks it's neat that the steel drums are made from empty oil cans. We hear their rhythms echo all over the island.

Music, sweet music!

My island has its own volcano.

Sometimes it sends puffs of smoke and fire into the air.

I wonder what it would look like if it erupted—but I wouldn't want to be nearby if it did.

Not far from the volcano is a wild, wild forest where we go fishing.

We don't want to scare the fish, so we stand there quietly and just listen to the bird songs and frogs and insects and the sound of the bubbling mountain stream.

Ding dong…ding dong.

Today's my cousin's wedding!

Lucca and I ring the church bells as hard as we can to let everyone know Yonnie and Sarieta are married.

Then we go to my aunt's house for a big party.

On the night before we go home, we get to stay up late. It's carnival!

Jump up!...Jump up!

Our toes barely touch the ground as we dance to the carnival songs that play all night long.

When morning comes, our visit to my little island is over.

Lucca and I don't want to say good-bye to my aunt and cousins and all our friends.

We just say, "We'll come back. Soon!"

"Isles Bay"

FOR MY FAMILY OF FRIENDS

Acknowledgments

Plates are from the following collections: "The Old Airport": Collection of Aleph Kamal; "Blue House on Wall Street": Collection of Jack and Linda McBride; "Market": Collection of Mr. & Mrs. Charles F. Grell; "Downtown": Collection of Mr. & Mrs. Charles F. Grell; "Salem Market": Collection of Kathy Schenker; "Fishing West Indian Style": Collection of Mr. & Mrs. Charles F. Grell; "St. Christopher's School": Collection of Dave and Rae Jonason; "Wedding": Collection of John Locke; "Carnival": Collection of Mr. & Mrs. Charles F. Grell; "Isles Bay Beach": Collection of Stewart Copeland.

Special thanks to Jane Parfet, Annie Woolley, Shona Martyn, Judy Astley, and Andy Summers.

My Little Island
First published in Great Britain by Macmillan Publishers, London and Basingstoke.
Copyright © 1984 by Frané Lessac
Printed in Mexico. All rights reserved.

Library of Congress Cataloging-in-Publication Data
Lessac, Frané
  My little island.
  Summary: A young boy goes with his best friend to
visit the little Caribbean island where he was born.
  1. Children's stories, American. [1. Caribbean
Area—Fiction] I. Title.
PZ7.L56283My 1984   [E]   84-48355
ISBN 0-397-32114-7
ISBN 0-397-32115-5 (lib. bdg.)
ISBN 0-06-443146-0 (pbk.)